P9-DFS-560

We Are Brothers

Text copyright © 2018 Yves Nadon · Illustrations copyright © 2018 Jean Claverie
Designed by Rita Marshall; edited by Amy Novesky · Published in 2018 by Creative Editions
P.O. Box 227, Mankato, MN 56002 USA · Creative Editions is an imprint of The Creative Company
www.thecreativecompany.us · All rights reserved. No part of the contents of this book may be
reproduced by any means without the written permission of the publisher. Printed in China
Library of Congress Cataloging-in-Publication Data
Names: Nadon, Yves, author. / Claverie, Jean, 1946– illustrator. Title: We are brothers / by Yves Nadon;
illustrated by Jean Claverie. Summary: In this sweet coming-of-age story bound up in summertime fun,
a younger brother discovers newfound resolve and joy, thanks to the encouragement of his older brother.
Identifiers: LCCN 2017021133 / ISBN 978-1-56846-292-9
Subjects: CYAC: Encouragement—Fiction. / Success—Fiction. / Diving—Fiction. / Brothers—Fiction.
Classification: LCC PZ7.1.N25 We 2018 / DDC [E]—dc23
First edition 9 8 7 6 5 4 3 2 1

3 1526 05134038 5

WITHDRAWN

We Are Brothers

Yves Nadon

illustrated by

Jean Claverie

Creative Editions

Here I am,
facing *the* rock.

From the water,
it seems even bigger
than in my memories.

Gray.

Immense.

Solid.

A wall!

Every summer, at our family's lake house,
my big brother and I swim to the rock.
Every year, he jumps off, as I watch and cheer,
too afraid to even try.

This morning, while my brother
and I were walking to the water,
he told me it was time. I was big enough.
"It's your turn now."

Not now, I thought.

I watch as my brother swims to the rock, climbs to the top, then runs and jumps without the slightest hesitation. He yells all the way down and splashes into the water beside me.

With force and grace, my brother had flung himself into the air. He always made everything look so easy. He is cat. He is bird. He is fish.

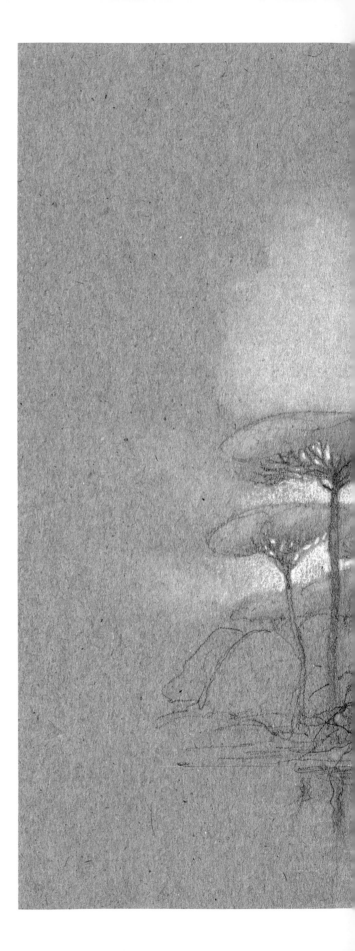

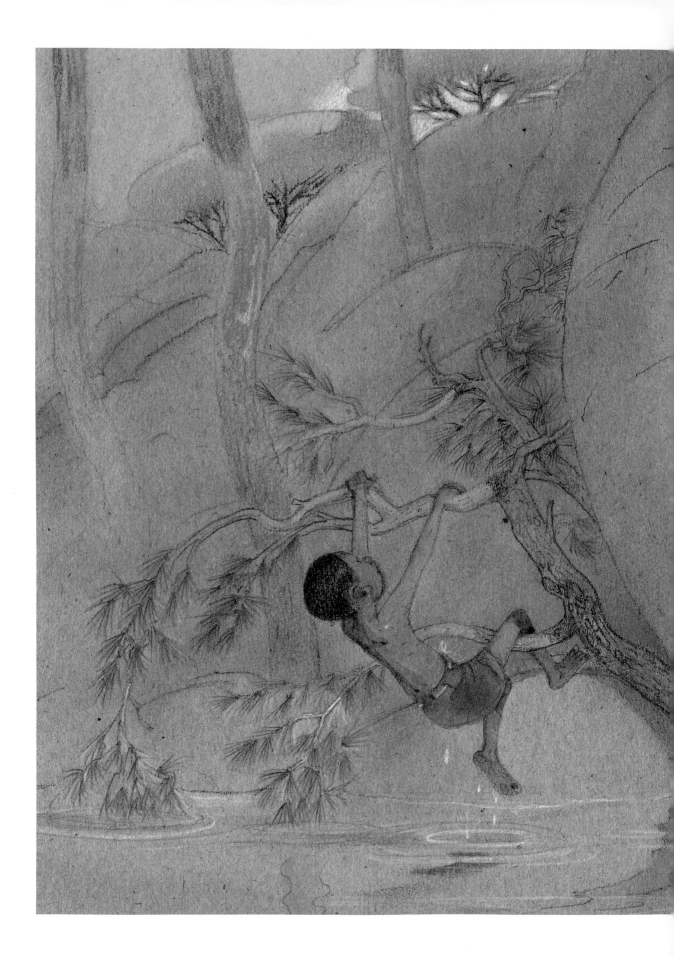

Not daring to show my fear, I gulp and swim to the bottom of the rock, where the pine branches touch the water. Nervously, I take hold of one of them and pull myself out of the lake. The tree branch feels warm and rugged, familiar and encouraging, even.

To my surprise, the path is so clear. Left hand on a root, right hand in a crevice, push with my left foot, grab a branch with my left hand, lift my right leg to stand on a slab, pull myself up with both hands on a big root, and stand on top of the rock.

I am cat.

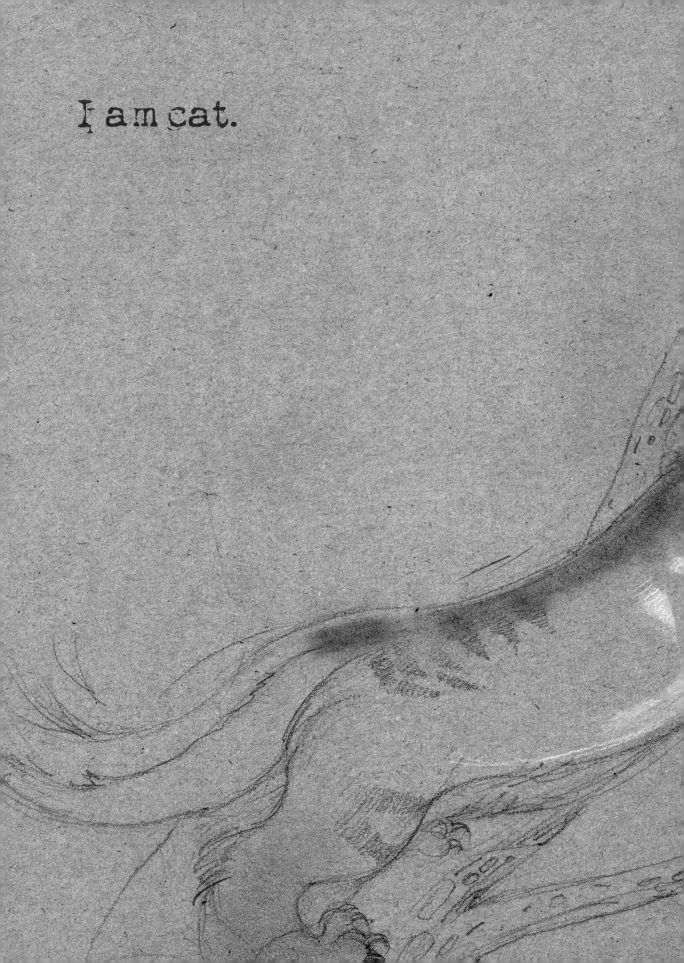

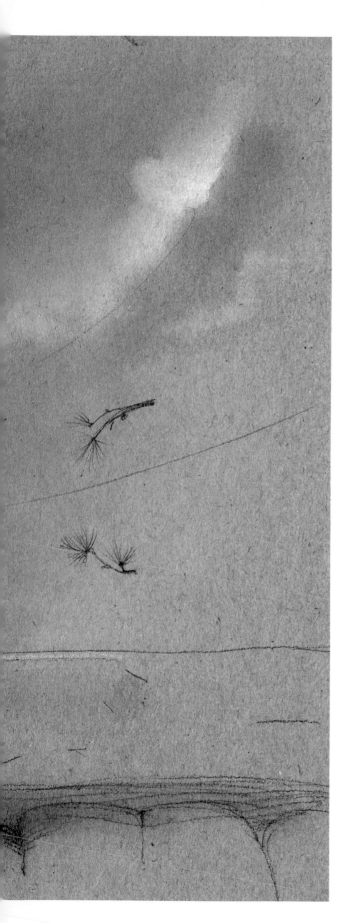

Legs shaking, turning around, the water seems so far away. Too far. A breeze makes me shiver.

But even from the top of the rock, I can see my brother's eyes, just above the water, believing in me.

Not now, I think.

What if I slip?
What if I miss?
What if I *die*?

Not now, I whisper.

Breath. Heart. Breath, breath, heart.
Breath,
breath,
breath.
My brother's eyes...
Heart.

Now!

I take a few steps back, run toward
the edge of the rock, and leap into
the sky. Everything seems to stop.
I am suspended in the air. All is
still, silent.

And then, I am yelling, my arms
circling, my legs running in the air.
My hands stretch for the sky, while
my feet call for water. My eyes find
my brother's.

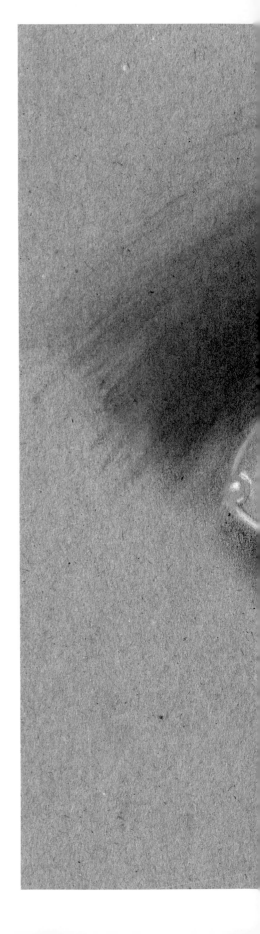

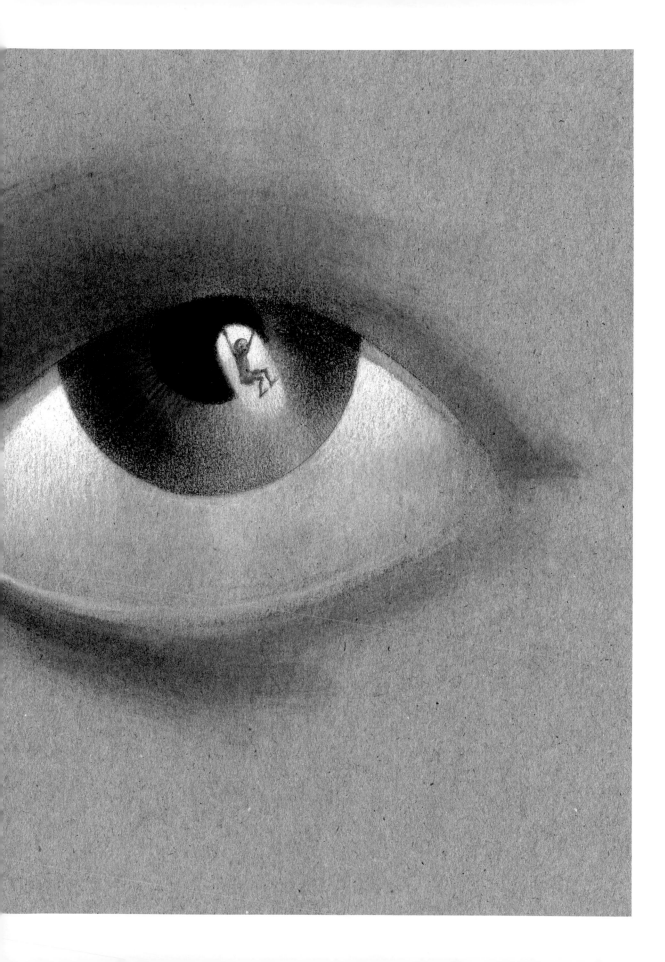

I am bird.

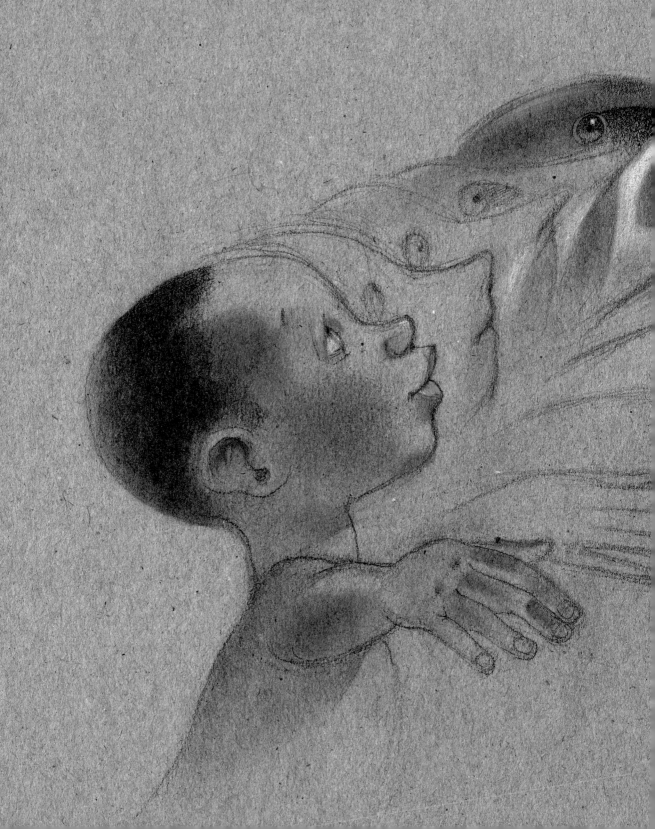

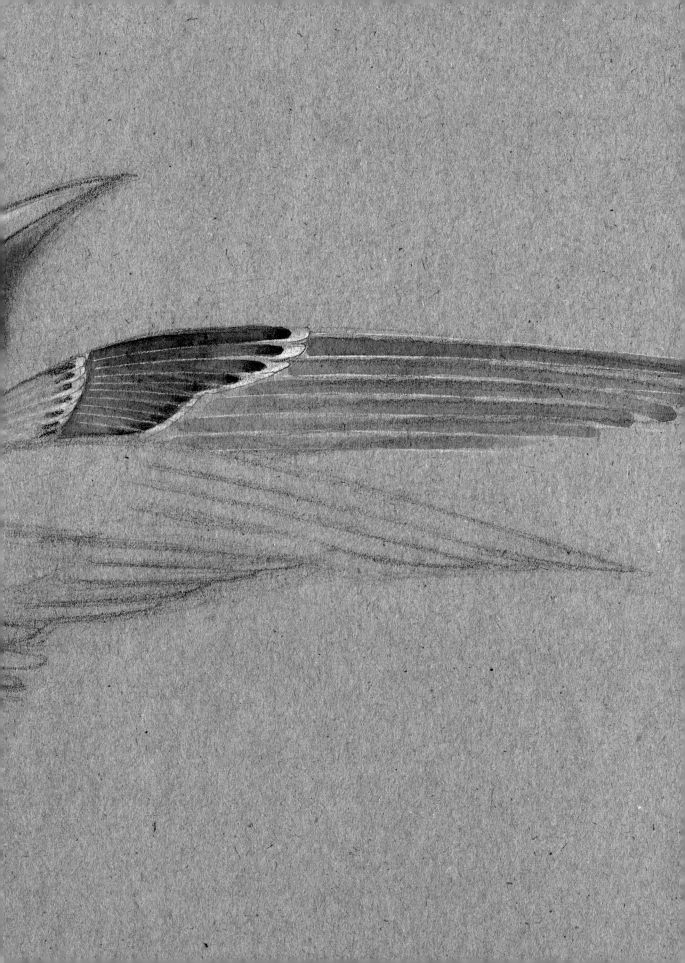

And water, all of a sudden.
I am bathing in the black
and the stars. I am alive.
I am home.

I am fish.

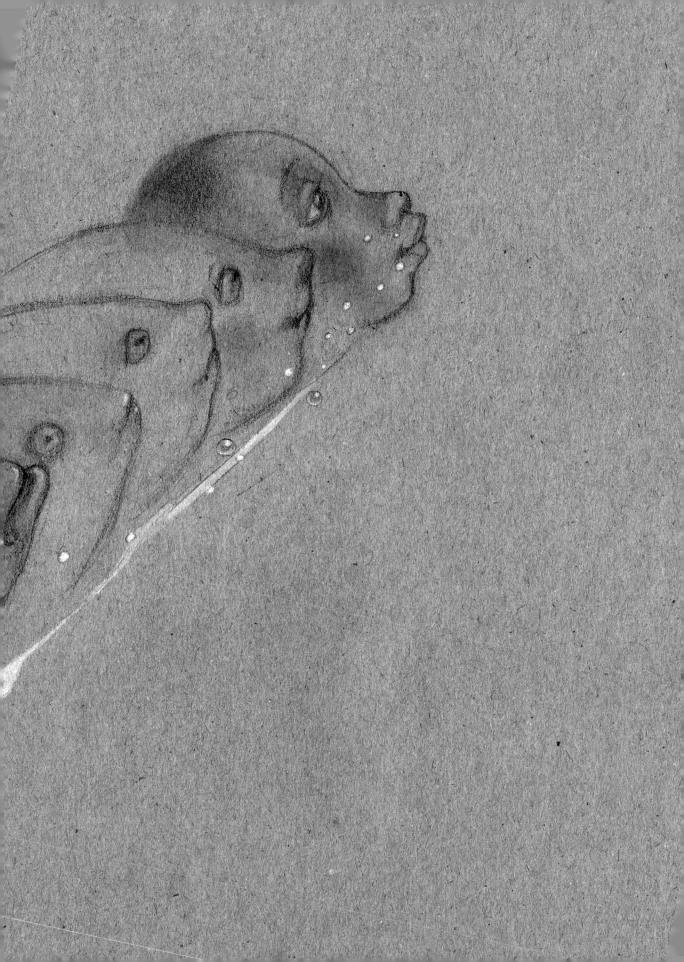

I break the surface and roar.

"You did it!" shouts my
brother.

He claps his hand in mine,
his eyes shining with pride,
and we both know what we
are going to do now.

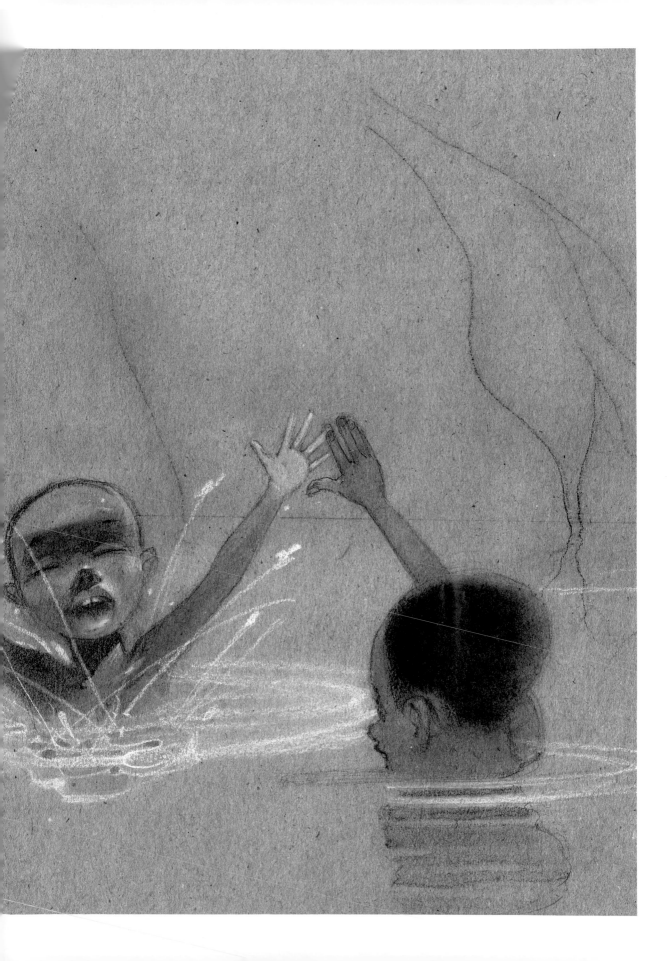

We are cat.
We are bird.
We are fish.

We are brothers.